THE KI

For Jane Gardam the best sound in the world is "a child laughing out loud at a book", and her books have been making children laugh and think for many years. Among her titles for young readers are the Walker Double *Black Woolly Pony, White Chalk Horse* and the Walker Story Book *Tufty Bear*. Her books for older readers include *A Few Fair Days* and *The Hollow Land*, which won the Whitbread Children's Novel Award. She has also won major prizes for her adult books. Jane Gardam is married with three grown-up children and lives in Kent in an old house, which has the ruins of a monastery and a chapel in the garden – and, some say, a ghost!

The Kit Stories

Written by
JANE GARDAM

Illustrated by
WILLIAM GELDART

WALKER BOOKS
AND SUBSIDIARIES
LONDON · BOSTON · SYDNEY

To Neville and Felicity

First published as *Kit* (1983) and *Kit in Boots* (1986)
by Julia MacRae Books

This edition published 1998 by Walker Books Ltd
87 Vauxhall Walk, London SE11 5HJ

2 4 6 8 10 9 7 5 3 1

Text © 1983, 1986 Jane Gardam
Illustrations © 1983, 1986 William Geldart
Cover illustration © 1998 Paul Howard

This book has been typeset in Plantin Light.

Printed in England

British Library Cataloguing in Publication Data
A catalogue record for this book is
available from the British Library.

ISBN 0-7445-5456-X

CONTENTS

KIT

KIT IN BOOTS

Kit

ONE

The Kit was not a kitten. She was a girl. She was seven and she was called The Kit because she was a baby. If you are a baby when you are seven – that is to say, if you are still crying over just this and that (such as juicy black beetles walking out from under the sink, or getting your new shoe in a clart) then you are a Kit.

Not if you cry over big things. Not if you cry over lambs going to market or the pig-killer coming. Farming fathers and mothers often mind about these things themselves even though they put on strong faces. Farming mothers often take their children down to the beck to wobble on stones and splash and put hands under ice-cold waterfalls or twizzle about in a rubber dinghy under low branches along the bank, when the pig-killer comes.

The Kit's mother did anyway.

But what mothers and fathers say round about The Kit's farm when a child cries for nothing is, "So this is The Kit is it?" They say it in voices that mean they don't think much of Kits.

When you are brave, however, and stop crying, and wipe your face up and give a stamp at the black beetles or sensibly take off your shoe and clean the clart away (a clart by the way is a cow-pat), then they say, "*That's* a good girl," and they half sing,

"Is this the *Cat*
That was the *Kit*
Before she went to *London*?"

The Kit, whose real name was Catherine, and Kitty for short, hardly ever got this said to her: for she really was a bit of a misery.

"I don't know why she's such a moaning minnie," her father used to say. "She's the dead opposite of our Lisa."

"Isn't she?" he used to add, tickling baby Lisa under the chin; and baby Lisa would wave her spoon and scatter mush about the carpet, and thunder her heels against the foot-rest on her baby chair, and girn like a monkey, and smear food on her scarlet cheeks, and laugh until her blue eyes nearly disappeared, and very messy The Kit thought she was.

Nothing seemed to upset Lisa. Once she even fell out of her chair on to her head and when they picked her up she was still laughing.

"There's my little cat," their mother had

said, hugging her. "My little cat's got to London already."

"Who wants to go to London?" said The Kit. She didn't know what London was but she knew that she didn't want to go to it.

She didn't want to go anywhere. She wanted to sit in the hay and eat apples, or make a cave in the bracken above the farm, and plant peas and carrots even if the sheep

came and ate them. She wanted to balance
about on the stone walls and pounce down
and watch the lambs leap in the air like
electric shocks; or creep up near the cows
and hear the huge tearing sounds they made
with their tongues, tugging out the grass.
She liked cows and they did not frighten her.
She even liked the bull rather, and used to
lean over the gate at him and stroke his huge

knobbly forehead, and he would blow loud noises at her and swing his head about. Her father would shout, "That'll *do* now," and come running, seeing her nearly toppling over the field gate. He would whisk The Kit up in his arms and roar at the bull who would roar back at him.

"I don't know," said The Kit's father, "I've known some daft youths, but never like this Kit. Cry, cry over midges and then goes stroking a demon like that Geoffrey!"

Geoffrey was the bull's name. He had bright, angry eyes all his waking hours, which seemed to be always. Even at night you could hear him thumping about in the dreadful, dark hull (a hull is a stone shed), which was supposed to be his bedroom but where he often spent his days too, and if The Kit crept up to peep through the hole in his door-sneck (a sneck is a latch), there was his slimy, rattly nose-ring and his pink, wet nostril half an inch from her eye. The Kit hated the bull's hull, and the bull's slimy nose-ring and the bull's pink, wet nostril, but she loved the woolly part of his nose and his forehead and tickled it through the sneck-hole very happily; and Geoffrey used to fling away and snuffle and shout like the baby did when their father tickled her chin.

"Leave over tormenting that bull," her mother would shout. "Come and help me jam these plums."

But The Kit hated jamming plums. They made her hands sticky and got everywhere, even on the soles of her shoes and then the shoes made crackling noises and left plummy tracks all over the kitchen floor, and her mother said, "Oh, give *over* then Kitty. Lisa could do better."

"She's got no sort of *gumption*," her

mother used to say at school to Miss Bell, but Miss Bell would say, "Nonsense Margaret." (Miss Bell had taught The Kit's mother too, long ago.) "I think that Catherine will give us a surprise one of these days." And she let The Kit sit at the back of the class and do Drawing in Reading – because The Kit could read like anything, anyway. The Kit would draw Geoffrey thumping about in a dark and dreadful cave, trying to get at the carrots and peas which the smug sheep were eating, his eyes giving off space rockets of despair.

Two

After a late, cold lambing, hay-time came early that year. Something magic happened to the weather and as early as March it grew hot as summer holidays – and hotter. The grass grew up bright and green. It blew in the warm wind, and turned golden and dry and not even too full of flowers for good hay. All kinds of jobs got left that were usually done in the pause after the lambs had come – like the straightening of the stone roof-slates which had slipped sideways in the wind; the building up of field walls knocked over by snow; and the small repairs to the farm buildings, like the door-sneck inside

17

the bull's hull which had come to the end of its life, after being eaten by frost.

"Are you going to mend that *sneck*?" The Kit's mother asked The Kit's father again and again. "It's a disgrace."

"It's no disgrace," said he. "It's lasted these hundred years. None of us is going to be as useful by that age."

"Well, it's no use at all now," said The Kit's mother. "It's sunk down in the muck of the hull – and that's another disgrace. It's three foot deep in muck, that hull, but it'd not take half a day to clear it."

"There's no half days to spare," said The Kit's father, sniffing the sky. They were all standing in the first big hay-field. The Kit was holding her mother's hand. The baby on her father's arm was bouncing and singing and conducting an orchestra. "I've the feel we could start hay any time. Even tomorrow."

"Well, that hull door isn't safe. It's going to give trouble."

"Never it will. It's only from inside you can't get out. There's no trouble from outside getting in. You can still shut the bull up safe, which is all that matters. It's no loss that he can't lift the latch on the inside himself, and get out."

"No – but someone else might want to lift the latch from inside to get out. Someone could get shut inside with him. Someone taking in his feed."

"Lunatics maybe."

"No. Not lunatics. Me. If you were away off somewhere and Kitty at school, I could be trapped in there, no one to hear me shout but the baby. There's often no one up here all day except the postman, and he doesn't come every day. I'd be trapped if that door swung to when I was feeding up. Or Kitty could be trapped if she was round there calling."

"She'd never go in, would you Kit? Not in that slathery muck of a hull."

"No," said The Kit, shivering, "I wouldn't. I hate the bull's hull. I just talk to him through the sneck-hole."

"There'll be no talking to anyone tomorrow, through sneck-holes or what-all," said her father. "It'll be all hands to hay-time."

And it was. For six days The Kit's parents and The Kit worked and worked. The Kit minded Lisa and ran back and forth to the field with sandwiches. She got Lisa in and out of her chair, and in and out of her play-pen, spooned her dinner in to her mouth, and washed her face afterwards. She made tea, put it in a can, ran to the field again with it, kept the stove going for hot water for baths, answered the telephone, fed the chickens and the pigs and the sheepdogs and watched her parents after they had fed the calves and the bull (which was grown-up work) falling asleep as they ate their own supper at night.

She didn't go to school. There was no question of that. All down the Dale other, richer

farmers were working, too, some of them with expensive machines in the fields and five and six helpers, but even in these fields there were quite big children missing school and working at the hay.

"Miss Bell'll be furious," said The Kit.

"She always was," said her mother. "Hay-time."

"She says it's slave labour," said The Kit.

"She always did," said her mother.

THREE

The weather was so wonderful that after six days of cutting and baling the hay, it was dry and sweet as lavender bags and The Kit's father said, "There's miracles about. I've never known a year like it. We can elevate tomorrow."

Elevating is lifting the hay blocks up into the stone barns for winter. Rich farmers – most farmers – have electric, caterpillarish machines for this and it is easy; but poor farmers have to toss the blocks up with a fork from a pick-up below. It is very hard work and gets harder as you get nearer the end, because the smaller the pile gets in the farmyard, the higher you have to toss it up. The Kit's father took over the hardest work right up to the finish, but, when it was nearly all done, The Kit and her mother who had been catching and stacking, which is very hard, too, looked out of the high barn door above his head with sore eyes and sneezing noses and aching arms and pitiable faces.

"What's this then?" said he.

"We're done. We can't finish. We've got to stop stacking," said The Kit's mother.

"Stand aside then," he said, and he tossed up the last bales. "Come on. Down the ladder and I'll up and finish them."

They came down the ladder and up went he, and in the dark of the barn he heaved and jig-sawed the last big, heavy bales of hay into place until all was tidy and safe, and the barn was full.

Then he took a step back to look at how

beautiful it all was and fell out of the high barn door in to the farmyard far below and broke his leg!

You never heard such a noise except perhaps from Geoffrey the bull when he'd been shut up in the hull too long in fine weather. The Kit's father was a big strong

man and when he fell on anything it was usually the thing he fell on that broke, not he. But farmyards don't break, and if this one had not still had a good layer of hay on it more of The Kit's father than just his leg would have broken, and he wouldn't have been able to roar at all.

The Kit's mother rushed to the telephone while The Kit hugged Lisa tight, and chickens, sheep-dogs, calves and Geoffrey clamoured for their supper in vain.

Soon from far away, The Kit could see the ambulance coming and then ambulance men walked firmly across the yard with a stretcher.

"Take away that stretcher," roared The Kit's father, "I'm not leaving this farm."

"You can't stay lying there in the hay," said the ambulance men. "You'll have broken something. You'll have to be x-rayed."

"X-ray me here," commanded The Kit's father with rolling, Geoffrey-like eyes, his beard twitching with rage and pain. The ambulance men talked together and went away, and soon another van was to be seen winding its way up the dale, with the Doctor's car ahead of it.

The Doctor took no notice at all of The Kit's father's roars – simply directed the x-ray men to help him into the house with him. Then, after the x-ray men had taken the photographs to the van to develop, and a lot of telephoning had gone on, and The Kit's father had said about a hundred times that he would not leave the farm, the Doctor said, "Very well – but if you stay here you'll not be able to move. Maybe not for six weeks. You'll have to be put in traction."

"Tied in my bed?"

"Yes."

"But where I can keep an eye on things?"

"We can really manage on our own—" said The Kit's mother.

"WHERE I CAN KEEP AN EYE ON THINGS?" roared The Kit's father.

"If you must," said the Doctor, "though I'm glad the telephone is halfway up the stairs, where you won't be able to get at it."

"Put me in traction then," he said, shutting his eyes and pointing his beard at the ceiling.

Then The Kit and Lisa and their mother went for a walk by the beck, far out of the way, and Lisa laughed the whole time and their mother cried and The Kit thought that this was being a very long day.

FOUR

"Six weeks," said the Doctor, when they got back. "It will be six weeks at the very least. More like eight."

"Margaret, have you fed that *bull*?" rang out from the big kitchen. They had put The Kit's father in the kitchen on a bed, to be near the centre of things and to save getting him up the stairs.

"No. Not yet. I —"

"He's not to move," said the Doctor. "But you needn't worry. He's tied by the leg so he can't stir. You can see. There's a big weight attached to him. You'll have no trouble. I've given him something to calm him down."

"HAVE YOU FED THEM ANIMALS?" bellowed The Kit's father.

"Not yet, for goodness sake!" wept her mother.

"I'll be round tomorrow. And every day," said the Doctor, "and bear up."

"Oh yes," he added by his car, pointing at The Kit, "this one's for school tomorrow. She needs a bit of peace."

"She's needed here," roared her father.

"She is *not*," said the Doctor.

"I can't manage without her. Not with the baby," said her mother. "Up here it's not like in a village. There's no neighbours."

"Oh, I'll stay," said The Kit, "I don't care."

"Well, I do," said the Doctor, "I say school."

And the next day she did go to school and Miss Bell was very glad to see her, but the day after that her desk was empty again.

For the magic weather had gone.

It was as if, when The Kit's father had fallen out of the hay barn, the sun had fallen out of the sky.

First of all a wind began to blow. Then great clouds came sweeping in from the head of the Dale and swirled all over it. Then the whole sky darkened and the real rain

31

began – great swinging curtains of it that turned the little roads into young rivers, the becks into brown torrents and the river down the Dale bottom into flood-waters which spread over the fields like pale, frothy lakes. At the end of the road, down from the farm, a rushing stream appeared in less than an hour, so deep that it covered the flimsy wooden foot-bridge that two days ago had been as dry as matches. "The bridge is covered," said The Kit, coming back from trying to go to school, "so I couldn't get."

"Oh dear," said her mother, very pleased. "Here then. Just get your father's breakfast while I get on with my washing. Though where to hang it out – round his bed in the kitchen, likely. If ever the Doctor gets here we'll get him to carry the television in here. It'll make evenings easier at least."

"I can't watch with *Father*," said The Kit.

"You'll have to or I'll run mad," said her mother. "Oh and when you've got his breakfast, set Lisa on her pot."

"Must I?"

"Yes, and why not Madam?"

"I hate it. I hate everything." She began to cry.

"Oh, heaven help us," wept her mother back.

"Bah, bah, bah, *hoop*-la," sang the baby.

"Where's my *breakfast*?" roared their father. "Have you seen to the calves? Will someone come here and scratch my foot – I've an itch to it."

"I won't, I won't," cried The Kit.

The kitchen steamed with wet washing, the rain bucketed down outside and neglected Geoffrey, in the bull's hull, swung his head and thought of murder.

FIVE

But it was over a fortnight later that the most fearful thing happened, just when you would have thought that everyone would have been settling down. The rain had turned to no more than a cold, fine mizzle, the Doctor was still coming once a week up the hill, though it had to be on foot, and, though no visitors had yet ventured up to the farm, the foot-bridge was quite possible in wellingtons. The Kit's father was not in so much pain and had begun to watch Breakfast Television, which he thought was marvellous, and the baby was as good as ever. Nicest of all, the people who telephoned from round about were full of praise for the whole family for being so clever as to get their hay safe in before the storm – "Grand young farmers," they said. "And even the little lass is helping."

The trouble came on a Tuesday morning when The Kit and her mother suddenly got furious with one another.

Neither of them knew how it started. Nor did The Kit's father, who for once was dumbfounded for nearly half a minute. Nor did the baby, who fell silent in the middle of a coo.

The truth is that The Kit and her mother had been crammed in too close to each other for too long and had grown a bit peculiar – rather like when you look at yourself in a mirror for a long time. They were both tired of the inside of the house and they both knew that The Kit ought to be back at school.

This drowning wet morning, with a bad-tempered wind blowing, The Kit had been told to go and get the pig bucket and take it to the pig, and she came running in to say that she had seen a shabby, wet rat eating out of it and she began to scream and cry.

"Rat!" roared her father, and her mother joined in, "Really Kitty – afraid of a rat! And you living on a farm. What if it was Africa with lions and tigers?"

"I *love* lions and tigers," The Kit stopped wailing to say, "I hate mucky, foul, filthy rats."

"That's enough, you're frightening Lisa."

"And messy, clever-*cats*." And she kicked the baby's bouncing-chair.

"That'll do!"

"And mucky, foul, filthy old *dumps*."

"Kitty!"

"Like this one. This farm. All mucky. And wet. Like the bull's hull. Like *you*."

And before anything could be done or said she was gone from the house, down the yard, through the trees and out of sight.

Silence fell in the kitchen.

After a moment or so her mother went to the window and then to the door and looked through the cold rain that blew in at her. "She'll be back," she said.

"Aye, she'll be back," said her father. "Daft young 'ape-orth."

The Kit's mother shut the door and dried her face and hair on a tea-towel, "Them rats," she said.

"There's rats everywhere," said The Kit's father. "Plenty in towns. London's full of them it's said. Only difference is you don't see them in London. They slink about secret. Underground."

"Well, that might be better."

"I'd sooner have things out in the open."

"I never liked rats," said The Kit's mother. "Nor yet dirt. Rats mean dirt."

"Never. There'll be rats in Buckingham Palace."

"That I'd doubt. Rats brought The Great Plague. D'you remember drawing it for Miss Bell?"

"Aye. But rats is natural beings. Live and let live. That Kitty's soft. She can't think."

"She's young yet for thinking," said her mother. "Mind that bull's hull *is* a sight. There's no way but I'll have to get on with cleaning it out myself I suppose."

"That you'll not. That I forbid," and The Kit's father began to thump the bed and thunder at his strung-up leg.

"Well, I'll have to feed and water the bull anyway," she said, "and the rest of them." She finished the washing-up and put on a scarf, a macintosh and a sacking apron over the macintosh. "I'll do the pig and calves and Geoffrey and then I'll away up to the gimmers." Gimmers are last year's lambs, teenagers, and often take quite a bit of seeing to, like teenaged people. These gimmers were on a high bit of fell over a mile away.

"I'll be a while," she said. "Are you all right? Kitty'll be back in a minute."

"Aye, as right as I'll be till I get these strings off." He lay back and closed his eyes. Lisa strapped in her chair had done the same and The Kit's mother riddled the stove, put on her wellingtons and went out.

She took the rat-eaten pig bucket and fed the pig. Then she make up the milk buckets and fed the calves.

She fed the chickens.

She went to the barn for the bull's fodder and the bucket of water to put in his trough. Both arms full, she went the hull. She had to kick the door open behind her to get in, and leave it standing wide, but she knew that the bull would make no move to get out with his dinner coming. "Hello Geoffrey," she said.

41

Geoffrey was standing quietly, up above his ankles in his treacly black carpet. He had a puzzled, thoughtful look, not unfriendly. He has his kindly side, she thought, he makes a lot of noise but he's a pleasant

enough young bull. She tossed hay up into the manger and Geoffrey came squidging across. He leaned against her for a moment and sighed and then began to eat the hay. "Poor lad," she said and scratched his iron forehead. "What a life. Shut up in here in the dark. Not even knowing it's not for ever. You don't even know if you'll ever get out in the fields again, do you young Geoffrey? Don't even know that things change and the sun comes out? And not a soul to talk to. No wonder bulls go mad." She scratched his thick, red, woolly neck as he stretched it up to the hay. "They say you can never trust a bull," she said, "not even one you've reared. But you're a grand lad, Geoffrey. You're right soft really." She stepped back, slipped in the deep mire, caught her wellington on the bucket, which clanged loudly as it fell against the water trough, and Geoffrey

43

reared away from the manger in fright.

At the same moment the wind slammed shut the broken hull door.

SIX

"I'm leaving," The Kit said to the foot-bridge, sploshing over it in her bedroom slippers. "*They'll* see. I'm leaving home. I hate them."

She sploshed on.

"I'm going," she told a big hay-lorry that came fizzing out of the dark rain along the main road, soaking her to the waistline.

"To London, since that's what they want," she informed the school gate, through which somehow or other she seemed to be walking.

"Oh good," said Miss Bell. "Dear me, Catherine, you're a bit wet. Let's take off those bedroom slippers. Did you not have a coat? Here, dry yourself and take off that dress. We'll find an overall."

"I'm all right."

"*Thank you*."

"Thank you."

"You're very late. We're halfway through Reading."

"Can I sit at the back?"

"No. Today you do what the others do."

She read, taking her turn round the class. She read very well, too, with lots of expression, though she felt cold and shuddery even in the overall. At Break she said, "Can I stay in?"

"No. The rain has stopped. You're all to go out. Today you do what the others do."

So she stood about the yard. When they said "Is your Dad's leg better?" she said, "He's all right." The sun came out and made the puddles flash in the yard.

It was over an hour later that her father in his kitchen bed woke up, tried to stretch, squawked, and saw the sun.

"No Kitty," he said.

The kitchen was flooded with light and all the drops along the gutter pipe outside the window were shining like wet glass beads. They kept scattering in the wind and new ones gathered up again. It'll be wild up on the fell with them gimmers, he thought next. Margaret's taking a time. They're *both* taking a time. Twisting his head to see the clock he found it was well after mid-day. By – they *are* taking a time. I must have been asleep near two hours. Lisa he saw was awake and watching him, and seeing him awake, began to biff her heels against her chair-rest and laugh. Then she began to biff them harder. Rather fiercely.

"Dare say you're getting hungry, young

47

lass, I know I am."

Outside the wind blew. Otherwise all was very quiet, for the bull's hull was a long way from the house.

At twelve-thirty, dinner-time, The Kit did not tidy up her books. When all the other children went pushing and shouting out of the room she sat on at her desk.

Miss Bell said, "Catherine?"

The Kit sat on.

Miss Bell came and sat at the next desk, and tears moved down The Kit's face.

"Is something wrong?"

"No."

"*No thank you.*"

"No thank you."

"Then go to your dinner."

"I went for my mother."

"I see. Today?"

"Yes. And they went for *me*. Both of them."

"I see."

"Then I ran away."

"Oh. I see. Then we must ring her up at once. She'll be very worried. She has plenty to worry about already. She'll have been on to the police by now."

"*She* won't worry about me." More tears rolled.

"I tell you, Catherine, that she will. I know

your mother. I've known her since she was seven like you, and she was as like you as a twin, except she was more of a scaredy-cat."

"My *mother*!"

"She was a proper scaredy-cat. Or Kit. She was the biggest Kit ever."

"My *mother*! She's strong and brave as lions."

"No she isn't. Now, Catherine, I've decided something. I'm not on dinner-duty and I'm free until afternoon school. I'll just have a word, and then we'll get in my car and we'll go up to the farm and we'll put things right."

"I'm never going back. Not to the farm. Never. I'm going to London."

"London'll keep," said Miss Bell. "Just at present you're going home."

SEVEN

They had to walk to the foot-bridge and Miss Bell, who was old, said that she had not walked this hill in years and hoped that she would never have to do so again.

"Though the trouble's worth it once you're up," she said, puffing and blowing as they came out on to the open pasture. Everything shone in the new sunlight and turned the bare hay-fields below to electric green and the heather common above to rich and furry people. The sheep stood bright and white, and the deep, muddy ruts in the lane shone silver. "Oh you live in a lovely place, Catherine," said Miss Bell.

"But whatever is *that*!" she said, reaching

for The Kit's hand.

A mixture of roars, howls, bellows and screams was rising from the farm and grew louder and louder as they hurried nearer. The Kit, rushing ahead into the kitchen, saw her father's rolling eyes and his hands desperately trying to free his broken leg from the Doctor's knots. Arching her back in her chair, black in the face, arms and legs spread, the baby was roaring at last.

But "Oh help!" said The Kit, for the really frightful noise was not coming from the house at all.

The Kit was gone.

"Jonathan," said Miss Bell sternly to The Kit's father, "What is this about?" But "Quick – Quick," he shouted at her. "Get to the bull's hull. Margaret's shut in there."

"No – no – get to the *yard*, woman," he roared as Miss Bell turned vaguely towards the wrong door, "Run!".

And Miss Bell ran, tottering a little on the flagstoned yard, slipping on the bumpy cobbles. For the first time in her life she felt watery and frail and old. And also for the first time in her life she felt that she didn't know quite what to do.

The awful noise had stopped. The only noise now was from inside – The Kit's father shouting and shouting, "I thought she was with the gimmers. She may have been an hour in there. Two hours. Why didn't she shout? It's only the bull you can hear. She'll be trampled! She's been trampled already! She's dead!"

And Lisa yelled.

Then there came a clumping, blundering noise from behind the hay barn and Miss Bell felt something else that she had not felt for a long time – fear. She could not move.

Around the corner of the barn, skidding in short zig-zags and fierce little runs came Geoffrey. He blew at the ground. His head swung. He turned his red eyes on Miss Bell who at once forgot she was old and frail and gave a great spring behind the dairy door – and bolted it.

Geoffrey put his forehead very near the ground indeed and began slowly, slowly to swing his head, he began slowly, slowly to scrape one of his front hooves backwards in a little trench. He gave a great bellow and prepared to charge.

Then quickly and quietly along the top of the wall from the direction of the hay barn came two black feet with two black ankles above them and The Kit above those. She skipped down out of sight into the hay-field and pulled the gate wide open – with herself well behind it. Geoffrey stopped scraping

his foot and stopped bellowing and slowly he lifted his head, blinked his crimson eyes and puffed a little down his nose. Then he sensibly trotted through.

The Kit bobbed up and shut the gate, was over it before Geoffrey could turn round, and found herself faced now with a wild and flying arms-aspread Miss Bell careering towards her like a huge, comforting pet goose. "Miss Bell," she said, "could you get Mother? She's halfway up the wall of the bull's hull and her macintosh and apron and scarf and that are all in the mire. She's clinging to the stones by her fingers and her toes are on the manger top and her eyes are all popping like a ferret. She can't speak for fright!"

"I'm sorry," she said, "I just can't go back. I hate that mucky bull. I know I'm a sop and I don't suppose I'll ever get to London."

"And I dare say you won't," said Miss Bell, wrapping her up in her wings, "I dare say you won't. For I don't see how any of them can do without you."

Kit in Boots

ONE

Kit was to be a bridesmaid.

She was to wear a dress of peppermint stripes. Pink and green. On her head was to be a hat like a bath-hat with a lace frill round it. On the frill would be bunches of pink and green ribbons. On her feet would be green satin slippers.

There they all were now, hanging from a nail in the ceiling of her bedroom. The nail stuck out from a black oak beam. Kit looked at the dress hanging, and the soft pretty hat and particularly at the green slippers every night as she fell asleep: and there they were again before her eyes as she woke up every morning.

Kit+dress+hat+slippers were all about to go to London, hundreds of miles away. Kit+dress+hat+slippers were all going to = one bridesmaid.

And this is how it had come about.

Kit was nine.

Long ago when she was six, out of her bedroom window one fine morning, she had

seen a glitter across the fields, far away from the farm in Bank Heads Pasture.

The glitter was metal. Motor-car metal. Few cars had been known to reach Bank Heads Pasture for it was very high with no proper road to it and it tipped down dizzily towards the river below. Also, Kit's father, the farmer, would have roared like his own terrible bull and eaten for breakfast anybody who dared to come and park a car on his land.

"Oh dear," said Kit.

Away she went out of the farm, past the sleeping sheepdogs who clanked their

chains a little as they raised their heads from dreams.

Away she ran across the yard, over the gate, down the lane to the gate of Bank Heads Pasture. No sign of the glitter yet. Down the hedge she hurried and the corn stood high. At last, by the bottom gate of the Pasture, in a corner with its back to her but facing the great view across the fields and moors was not only a car but a silver caravan, and a delicious smell of bacon.

Oh help, thought Kit.

She ran to the caravan and put her head round it. Sitting on a stool, holding a frying pan over a furious little blue cooking-stove, sat a gentle, tall man with long, fair hair. He was watching the bacon in the pan and smiling at it as it fizzed and popped at him.

"Good morning," said the tall man, not looking round. "Will you join me for breakfast?"

Kit said nothing and the bacon sizzled. She ran back fast and when she reached the farmyard saw her father blinking his eyes and rubbing both hands about in his hair and yawning at the blue day.

"Early about," he said to Kit.

"There's a caravan," she said, "in Bank Heads Pasture. With a man frying..." but before she could say "bacon" her father's hands had come out of his hair and his eyes had turned to flame.

"Caravan?"

"I don't know how ever it got there. He looks quite..." but before she could say "nice" her father had gone springing away, spitting like the bacon, thundering out of sight down the lane leaving roaring noises behind him.

"Oh dear," said Kit's mother. "What now? Campers? Do you want a cup of tea?"

She and Kit sat drinking tea and her sister,
Lisa, lay on their mother's knee smacking
her lips over her bottle of milk and rolling
her eyes about and dabbing at her mother's
cheek with a fist the size of a smallish rose.
Their mother looked gently down at Lisa.

"I wonder why he so hates people coming
up here?" asked Kit.

"It's his own land. He's had to work hard
for it."

"He might just let people sit on it now and then. They're doing no harm."

"He thinks they're having holidays. Work is all your father thinks about. He thinks caravanners are drifters. What was this one doing?"

"Smiling and cooking bacon. And looking at the view."

"There you are then. Your father'll slice him up. He'll turnip him through the shredder. In ten minutes that car will be starting up and the caravan will go bowling down the hill."

"Yes," said Kit, sadly.

The man had had such a different face. Different from anyone in the Dale. Long, like a horse, and narrow, like a bird, and little gold glasses on the end of his long nose. His hands were narrow and hard and clever-looking and he had sat so still and pleasant.

"Oh well," said Kit, watching through the window to see the glittery van pass out of her life.

Two

But half an hour went by and it was half-past seven and time for Lisa to be put back to bed and Kit to help get breakfast. The gold sun shone into the kitchen. Although it was nearly September it was quite hot. Foxgloves and red rowan berries seemed to be on fire. Kit stood on the step eating bread.

"Eat at the table. Are you a cow?" asked her mother.

"I'm looking for Father. It's very quiet."

"Cornflakes," said her mother. "At the table. Now."

"Oh look," said Kit. "He's there all the time."

Below the house, to the left of the lane, was the orchard. It was only three apple-trees, their old trunks flaky with silver velvet and a few blackcurrants with moth-holes in the leaves. The farm was so high that fruit would hardly grow at all, so the orchard was neglected. It brought in no money. But this morning, here was her father walking

through it towards breakfast. He looked stern, but quite calm and quiet.

"Good apples," he said, putting down some bitter little crimson ones on the table.

"What about the caravan?"

"Oh – nothing."

"What d'you mean, nothing? Was Kit sleep-walking? Dreaming?"

"No, no. It's there."

"Did you send them packing?"

"No, no. It's just one bloke. He's harmless. Just some Lonesome Jones."

Kit very much longed to take another look in Bank Heads Pasture on the way to school but there was no time. Nor was there time on the way home. But the next morning off she went again when she woke up, walking carefully this time, without a sound, approaching the caravan from the other side of the hedge.

70

The man was painting. He had an easel beside him and a box of squidgy paints in dark-silver tubes all twisted up like worms in pain, and a jar of brushes. This time there was a smell of paint, not bacon, and Kit drank it in and closed her eyes in glory.

"Good smell," said the man, again without looking round. "Paint is my petrol. Smell of life. You must be Kit."

"Did Father tell you? Did he talk?"

"This and that," said the man.

"It's a lovely picture," said Kit. "It's not a bit like our view, but it's lovely."

"Half shut your eyes and look again."

"Oh yes," she said. "It's coming on. Have you come from far away?"

"London," said the man.

"I've never been to London."

"You're still Kit in Boots, not Puss in Boots," he said.

"My father says you're Lonesome Jones."

He liked that, and smiled to himself as he went on with the painting. "There now. Light's gone. Have to leave it till tomorrow."

"But the light's just starting."

"No. It changes all the time. The light I'm painting has moved off. Stand still, Kit in Boots and I'll draw you."

Kit looked at her legs in muddy wellingtons. "I shouldn't bother with the boots," she said. "They're any old boots."

"No boots are any old boots. No leg is any old leg. I want to draw the space anyway."

"What space?"

"Where the leg goes into the boot. There's space all round. Like a cave. The boot is a cave."

"You mean you're drawing bits of dark now?"

"That's it. There you are."

Kit looked at Kit. For six she was a tall girl, very skinny. The stick legs went into the boots straight. Straight silk hair hung down her back and her face looked out of the picture at Lonesome Jones with steady eyes.

"It's me all right," said Kit.

"You can have it," said Lonesome Jones. "Take it home."

"Is it a present?"

"No. It's pay. I'd like a bucket of water."

"Oh, I'll bring it. I'll bring it now."

"I'll come and get it. Leave it by the orchard."

"Won't you come in for a cup of tea?" called Kit's mother. "It's just this minute made." It was five mornings later and the painter was collecting his bucket. He waved at her and smiled and shook his head and went away.

"Can't think how he puts his time in," said Kit's father a fortnight later. "He's quieter than an animal. Quiet as a hare."

"He looks a bit like a hare," said Kit. "And he's got eyes at the back of his head like a hare. Maybe he's a wizard."

"Then keep your distance," said her mother who was cross about the painter not wanting any tea.

"I'm watching him, don't you fret. I'm watching him," said Kit's father. "I take a

look over the gate mornings and evenings."

At the end of the next week when he was taking his look, he found an envelope with a five pound note in it pinned to the gate of the Pasture and the caravan and the car and Lonesome Jones all gone. When he got back to the farm he found Kit and her mother examining sheets of white paper they had found in the dairy. They were pictures of him, of Kit's mother and Lisa, the dogs on their chains, a muscovy duck, some sheep and a cow and the terrible bull, the three velvet apple trees, the farm-house with the

wind round it and all the curtains trying to fly out of the windows. There was a new one of Kit in Boots, too.

"He *has* worked hard," said Kit's mother.

"Work – rubbish," said her father. "Enjoying himself. Good to be some folk. I expect he's on the dole. They ought to be in prison, these vagrants. Stop gazing, Kit, and get those calves fed before school. We've a living to earn here."

I'll never see him again, thought Kit.

THREE

But she did. A year later he was back. And the next year. And the next. Always he came to the same corner of the Pasture, always at the same moment of the year. "Like the swallows," said Kit's father. He didn't much like swallows. They had such a carefree time, sweeping about the sky and having fun. He didn't think much of birds you couldn't eat. You couldn't eat holiday-making swallows just as you couldn't exactly eat Lonesome Jones.

Yet, although every year he would set out with a ferocious look towards the caravan, he always came back from it looking rather calmer, and Lonesome Jones stayed on.

One evening Kit went with her father to see if the Pasture was ready for cutting and they stopped beside the caravan. Lonesome Jones was nowhere to be seen.

"I think he's off, painting down the Dale," said Kit.

"Now stand back," said her father. "Don't go prying about."

"I'm not," said Kit who was standing over by the hedge. "I wouldn't. He's private."

"We've no rights to go interfering with

other people's lives," said her father, putting his eye against the caravan window. "Think how we'd feel if he came looking in at us."

"I know," said Kit.

"I've every right to keep an eye on him, mind." Her father swivelled his head about. "He might fire the cornfield with that stove. Hello." He had moved to another window and could see inside the caravan more clearly. "Well bless me!"

"What?"

"Nothing. There's nothing inside. It's like a caravan in a show-room. Not a radio or a can of beer or any food lying out. Not a fridge, no clothes. Just a blanket folded and the bucket and a plate and a kettle. Well, I'm not one to pry."

"No."

"By, he's poor. He must be rare and poor."

"See to it he has eggs and butter and

81

milk," he said to Kit's mother. "There's some terrible poverty in this world. Yet he's a proud man. He keeps himself clean as any of us."

Lonesome Jones accepted the food but always paid for it and each year at the end of his visit, which always happened without warning – suddenly the field was empty – there was what he called his rent in the dairy. Some of the pictures were so lovely that Kit's mother drove down to Leyburn to get them framed and hung them on the kitchen walls. "It's the painter from the caravan," she said. "Lonesome Jones."

"He's a lovely painter," said the butcher's van.

"He's got you all to the life," said Old Fishpool from over Redmire.

"He's a trained artist," said Kit's school-teacher, Miss Bell. "Did you not ask his name? There's many years of work behind a talent like that."

"Work," said Kit's father, toiling about under a huge hay-bale with a suffering expression and a tuft of hair sticking up from a hole in his hat.

"There's work and work," said Miss Bell. "There's work in the top storey and you never did much of that when I had to teach you."

"Muscle work's what counts," said Kit's father.

"My father says only muscle work counts," said Kit to Lonesome Jones next summer. She was eating hard pears on his caravan step. Between the bites she was drawing. "Miss Bell says it's school work that's work."

"Different sets of muscles," said Lonesome Jones. "For different things."

"Are there head-muscles?" asked Kit.

"I expect so. You need to know the right muscles for everything. Like learning to swim. And you have to learn not to use two sets at once sometimes. If you're drawing you use finger-muscles and if you're eating pears you use jaw-muscles. That could be a good drawing if you paid it some attention. Put down the pear."

Kit did and began to draw lovely pictures soon. Lonesome Jones asked to keep some.

"Will you all come to London?" he asked suddenly, the summer Kit was nine. "I'd like to show you some pictures."

"Can you imagine my father in London?"

"No," said Lonesome Jones. "Pity."

"I'll come one day," said Kit. "I'd love to. I've always wanted to. And look grand in London clothes. I'm down to Mum's niece's old bridesmaid's dress for best now and it's a thousand years old. All slimy satin."

"When I get married you can be my bridesmaid if you like," said Lonesome Jones.

"Aren't you a bit old for getting married?" asked Kit.

"That's what I have to decide," said he.

FOUR

The wedding invitation arrived before Christmas and Kit's father stood looking at it this way and that at the kitchen window as the first snow of winter came fluttering down outside. A paper fluttered out from the envelope, too, and Kit's mother picked it up.

"Kit a bridesmaid?" she said. "But we don't know him."

"Out of the question," said Kit's father. "Bridesmaiding out of the family! It's not our way."

"It's to be very pretty clothes," said Kit's mother. "There's a drawing. I'm to make them. I'd like that, now the evenings are darkening in and the telly's on the blink."

"In London. It's to be in London. Great guns – think of the train fares. They're the price of a heifer."

"Pink and green and white. Pink buttons Green shoes. They'll send the green shoes if we tell the size and draw round her feet. And they'll send the material."

"We could go by car. It's cheaper," said Kit.

"We have no car. We have a pick-up and a beast-trailer. And even in a car we could lose ourselves in the size of London. We'd reach the wedding late and be a shame before all. Anyway – we couldn't leave the farm. Too much work."

"It's before lambing."

"Too much work."

"It's after the sowing. It's the slack time, that early in the Spring."

"Work's never finished on a farm. Out of the question."

In the end it was arranged by Miss Bell,

Kit's school-teacher who was old and had taught Kit's mother and father, too, that Kit and her mother and the baby would go to London together on the train: one and a half, the baby going free – and that Kit's father would be left behind to take care of the farm, with some telephone numbers in case of loneliness and a full deep-freeze in case of blizzards. Miss Bell would take Kit and her mother and the baby to Darlington railway station on the Friday morning and meet them again on Saturday night. They would stay the night before the wedding with Miss Bell's cousin's daughter's niece just outside London and she would take them to catch the train home after it. Kit's mother and Kit turned pink and silent with joy when Miss Bell told them what was going to happen.

"All settled," said Miss Bell, glaring at

Kit's father and putting on her hat, and he made a noise like a distant storm and stamped off up the Dale.

When the peppermint-striped material arrived for the bridesmaid's dress, Kit's mother bought new scissors in Leyburn and began to be very happy and Kit who had already written to Lonesome Jones accepting the invitation, wrote again (with illustrations) to bring him up to date with all the arrangements and the latest news. She practised bridesmaiding up and down, up and down, in her bedroom, holding the bride's train and bowing to everybody left and right.

"Poor Lisa," she said to her sister after Christmas. "It's hard to be so young. It's a good thing you can't be jealous yet."

Lisa, who these days was not exactly being the angel that she had been when she was born, listened carefully and then turned her dinner out of its bowl on to the table and put the dish on her head like a rat.

"Lisa's very fratchity," said her mother the week of the wedding, "I hope she's not sickening."

"She feels all the commotion,"

said her father. "It's the pandemonium in the house. Everything breaking up around us."

"It's only for two days," said Kit's mother. "Kit, would you turn off that music and stop pacing about and come and see to Lisa for me. I'm getting nothing done. There's my own dress to finish. I've three last buttons."

Lisa pulled the cat's tail. The cat yowled and flew at the window-sill which was behind the cooker so that her front paws overturned the soup. Lisa plopped down on the rug and began to wail, and when they had mopped up the soup, stroked down the cat and sewn on the buttons, they saw that Lisa had lain down on the rug, curled into a twist with a fretful thumb in her mouth and her eyes very much too bright.

"She's hot," said Kit's mother.

She and Kit did not dare look at each other. They put Lisa to bed and that evening Kit could not even look in the direction of the suitcase which was already carefully packed in the hall with the green slippers just showing.

In the morning Lisa was covered all over in big red spots and so hot that her father said you could warm your hands at the cot-side. "So that's it," he said, his face a queer mix-up of worry and delight.

"What's it?" asked Miss Bell, arriving with her truck to take them to the station.

"Outing's off," said Kit's father. "Chicken-pox. The baby has chicken-pox

and Margaret can't leave her."

"And what about Kit? Is she to miss all?"

"Well, she can't go alone. We don't know the people. Vagrants and gypsies. I was never happy about it. It's a blessing in disguise. This chicken-pox has probably been sent."

"Rubbish," said Miss Bell.

"Oh, Miss Bell," said Kit's mother. "Oh, couldn't you take —"

"No I could not," said Miss Bell. "I've a garden crying out for manure and all my lessons to prepare for Monday."

"But I can't leave Lisa."

"Of course you can't."

"And Kit can't go alone. It's true. We really don't know these folk at all. They might turn out to be kidnappers."

"Of course Kit can't go alone," said Miss Bell, looking hard at Kit's father. "Not *alone*. It would be almost as bad as alone but at least she wouldn't get kidnapped."

"You're not thinking...?" and Kit's father's

eyes turned orange and his face turned very pale.

"Perhaps it might be in some ways *more* dangerous than being alone," said Miss Bell. "But sometimes we must live dangerously. Margaret, where is Jonathan's best suit?"

"It … it's in the wardrobe."

"Into that suit," said Miss Bell. "And be sharp. We've an express train to catch."

And on the fast train to London two hours later, sat Kit on one side of a table for four, with the suitcase and the wedding-present (a complete cheese) beside her; and across the double seat opposite spread her father in wonderful apricot-coloured hairy tweed and all his red curls springing up from his head like a prize highland bull.

"Four tickets needed here," said the ticket collector, but he hurried off to the next table when he saw the look in Kit's father's eyes.

"Oh don't worry so," said Kit. "It's supposed to be fun." She began to draw things in her notebook.

Her father looked out of the window at all the farmland they were passing and all the lovely work that he could have been doing on it.

"Seems right sinful sitting here," he said.

FIVE

They stood on the London station with the cheese and the suitcase, and people whirled and ran about and butted them and shoved them, and elbowed them out of the way. Some had black faces like Swaledale sheep, and some had white faces like Leicesters, and some had brown faces like Jacob's Ewes. It was like dipping-time when the flock goes jittering and bleating about as if they are all about to die. And there was not even a shepherd here. Kit and her father stood still in the midst of the flock. It thinned a little in time but there was no sign of Miss Bell's cousin's daughter's niece.

"We wouldn't know her anyway, would we?" asked Kit.

"I've seen her once at a funeral," said her father. "She's rather the sort you see at funerals. I never forget a face. You get practice with sheep. If you can tell one sheep from another you can usually tell one human from another. *Usually*," he said. "This place is going to be a test. And they're all in such a turmoil and a pother. Maybe there's a Fair on. Now then. There's a face I do know."

Lonesome Jones was standing peering through the steel mesh of the ticket gate.

"I thought I'd come along," he said. "Your lift is waiting outside the station but I thought you might like to see a well-known face. What's this, Kit? Drawings?" He took the notebook from Kit and sat down on a luggage-trolley and peacefully began to look at them, one after another.

"Cheese," said Kit's father. "We've brought a cheese," and a fat, bouncing lady with black eyes and a dress as green as a parrot came prancing up and swept Kit into her arms and twirled her about.

Help, thought Kit. She's not a bit like Miss Bell.

"I'm the bride," said the lady. "I'm Rosie. And Kit – you have really and truly arrived in London," and she tried to hug Kit's father too, and twirl him about but he stood very steady.

"We shall see you tomorrow," she cried as Miss Bell's relations, who were looking rather thoughtfully at Rosie, who was doing

a dance on the kerb, prepared to drive away. "Goodbye. Tomorrow is the day," sang Rosie and "Not bad in the least," said Lonesome Jones, looking up from the last drawing. "The head-muscles are flexing up at last, Miss Kit in Boots."

"Boots my foot," said Rosie and roared with laughter at the frightful joke. "She'll be Kit in silks tomorrow."

"What unusual people," said the kind relations of Miss Bell, with stony faces, and

Kit longed and longed for tomorrow to come. Which of course it did as tomorrow does and then it was over as tomorrow always is, too, and Kit's head-muscles and heart-muscles and all her muscles were flopping like the ribbons on her hat.

"It's all over," she said. "Oh, it's over" – for they were back on the train.

It seemed a second later.

They had arrived at the studio, they had gone to the church. The dress had been

perfect and so had the hat and so had the green slippers. She and three other girls all dressed the same (except that Kit's dress had much, much better sewing) had all carried bunches of daisies. The people had all gasped with pleasure to see them in their peppermint stripes, and taken lots of photographs. Rosie, the bride, had been the rosiest bride anyone had ever seen and had worn pink as bright as the daisies, and Lonesome Jones had worn a wonderful suit of pale grey with a purple silk waistcoat that had belonged to his great-grandfather, and although he had seemed very far away, and had looked around the roof of the church a good deal and squitted up his eyes as if he was thinking of painting it, he had answered the questions quite correctly. Yes, he would love Rosie forever and take care of her.

And all the bells rang.

Six

Afterwards at the party, which was at the top of a high white building in a picture gallery, with his paintings hanging round the walls, Lonesome Jones stood smiling and happy with his friends around him.

"Are you all right?" Kit asked her father. He was alone by the door, huge, like Samson thinking of pulling down the temple. "Isn't it wonderful? Isn't the food wonderful? Don't the pictures look wonderful – in the shiny frames. And the razzle-dazzle lights. And isn't the carpet thick? Some of the pictures are of us."

"I'm thinking of that caravan," said her

father, "and us offering him food and pitying him for poverty. And bringing that cheese. We've been made fair fools of today, Kit. The prices on those pictures! Hundreds of pounds."

"Some of them – most of them – are of you," said Kit, but she had to leave her father because one of the other bridesmaids pulled her away.

Later she saw her father talking to people and people going up to him and shaking his hand. Lonesome Jones stood beside him and Rosie piled his plate with lovely food and filled up his glass. And the noise and the laughing grew louder and the view from the window high above London – the towers and the dark domes and the spires and the coloured advertisements flickering, and the

little boats and barges sliding crooked far below along the River Thames – all grew blueish then shadowy, then violet, and lights began to twinkle out for miles and miles and miles.

"Time for you to go, the car is here," said Rosie. "Thank you for being such a good bridesmaid and for bringing us your father. He's a famous man, you know. His face is going to live for ever. Will you come and see us again?"

"I'd like to stay here always," said Kit.

"Wouldn't you miss the country?"

"I like all kinds of places," said Kit, "I'm different from my family. My father's hardly left the farm all his life."

"You live where your work is," said Lonesome Jones, "unless you're lucky enough to be a painter. Then you can live anywhere in the world."

Kit's father advanced on Lonesome Jones with a hand which was as beautiful with work as the pictures of it on the wall.

"Well, thank you for the hospitality," he said in a voice that said much more. Then to Kit's astonishment he added, "I wouldn't have missed it for the world."

"We'll see you in the summer," said Rosie. "I'll be coming, too, now."

"We'll find her some boots," said Lonesome Jones, and to Kit, "Open your bridesmaid's present in the train."

It will still all be over. All, all over, she thought.

But inside the parcel was a box of paints, a block of thick paper and a little soft bundle of charcoal wrapped in tissue, and Kit began to draw.

"That's right," said her father opposite on the two seats, behind a vast yawn. "Best mind those clothes though. You'll be back in your boots tomorrow."

But Kit thought nothing of that. As the train flew northwards, back to everyday, she sat in her peppermint stripes and with her green slippers tucked under her. She drew and she drew and she drew – all that she could remember of what she had seen and done.

"That's the way. Work hard," said her father, falling asleep. "Work hard. There's nothing like it."